The Yawn that Went around the World

The YAWN
that Went
around the
WORLD

By Patty
Labriola

& Dayna
Pappalardo

Illustrations by
Kathleen
Gurchie

NEW YORK

LONDON • NASHVILLE • MELBOURNE • VANCOUVER

The Yawn that Went around the World

Published in New York, New York, by Morgan James Publishing. Morgan James is a trademark of Morgan James, LLC. www.MorganJamesPublishing.com

Proudly distributed by Ingram Publisher Services.

Morgan James BOGO™

A **FREE** ebook edition is available for you or a friend with the purchase of this print book.

_____

CLEARLY SIGN YOUR NAME ABOVE

Instructions to claim your free ebook edition:
1. Visit MorganJamesBOGO.com
2. Sign your name CLEARLY in the space above
3. Complete the form and submit a photo of this entire page
4. You or your friend can download the ebook to your preferred device

ISBN 9781631959318 paperback
ISBN 9781631959325 ebook
Library of Congress Control Number: 2022935952

Cover and Interior Design by:
Kathleen Gurchie

Morgan James is a proud partner of Habitat for Humanity Peninsula and Greater Williamsburg. Partners in building since 2006.

Get involved today! Visit MorganJamesPublishing.com/giving-back

Patty Labriola:

Dedicated to all the children in my life, past and present, to whom I am "Aunt Patty" and "Grandma," but especially to the one who calls me "Mommy." Special thanks to my husband who helps make all my dreams a reality, and to our God who has and still makes all things possible.

Dayna Pappalardo:

I would like to dedicate this book to my incredible husband, my best friend and sweetheart, Vinny Pappalardo, who has always been my rock, ultimate encourager, and hero. I would also like to thank my beautiful children, Tony and Danielle, and their spouses, Frances and Dennis, for all the laughter, support, and love you have always given to me. My precious grandchildren are the sunshine in my life. This book was written for each of you. Always share your smiles.

Kathleen Gurchie:

To my love, Al, who is there for me throughout every project with his quiet strength and humor.

Yawns are so **FUNNY**—
you'll see what I mean.

Nobody *throws* one—

you **catch** one,
it seems!

It was a **sunshiny day**, like so many others,
And the story begins with me and my mother.

Mommy and I
were both in the car.
We were **going to town**;
it was not very far.

I'd missed my nap and was rubbing my eyes,

when I **yawned real big** as a taxi drove by.

"Oh no!" said Mother.
"Did you cover your mouth?
Or your yawn might
travel from **north**

to **south**!"

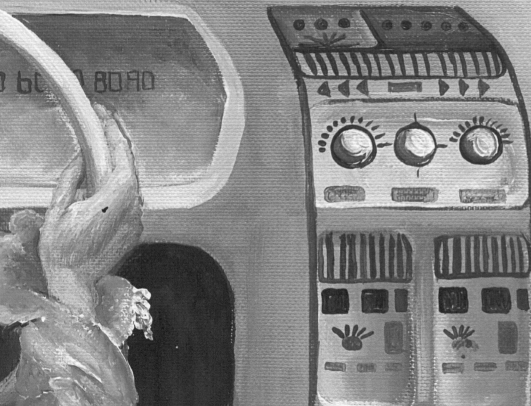

A man in the cab out the window was glancing;
he was going to Spain to **practice his dancing**. And just when I thought,
What a yawn, oh my, the man in the cab let out a **BIG SIGH**.

He arrived at the airport with no time to spare,
and before very long he was **high in the air**.

It was really too late; my yawn had been *SENT*.
Like an airmail package—**off it went!**

A flight attendant **caught** his yawn; she had been flying from dusk 'til dawn.

She **passed** her yawn to the folks on the plane: a doctor, a gardener, a teacher from Maine.

A skater from Russia who'd settled to rest, yawned so many times that her sleep was all *messed*.

There was a designer who made **pretty clothes** who brought yawns to Paris with **buttons and bows**.

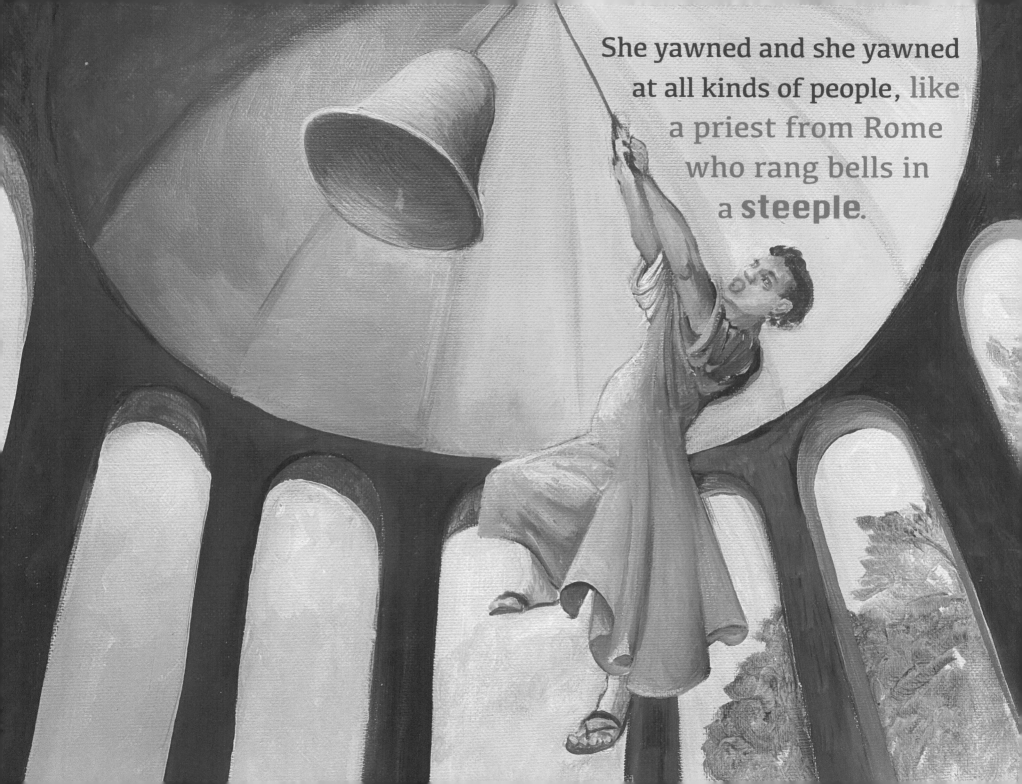

She yawned and she yawned
at all kinds of people, like
a priest from Rome
who rang bells in
a **steeple**.

A delegate yawned, then made his connection,
to the **Capitol Building** in time for election.

From country to country
my yawn would **TRAVEL**—

ANCHORAGE

BUDAPEST

HONG
KONG

BOMBAY

LOS
ANGELES

and, like a pull in a sweater,
would quickly unravel.

SYDNEY

But it was the last straw when,
later that night, just before we
turned out the light,

the President
was giving a
speech on TV...

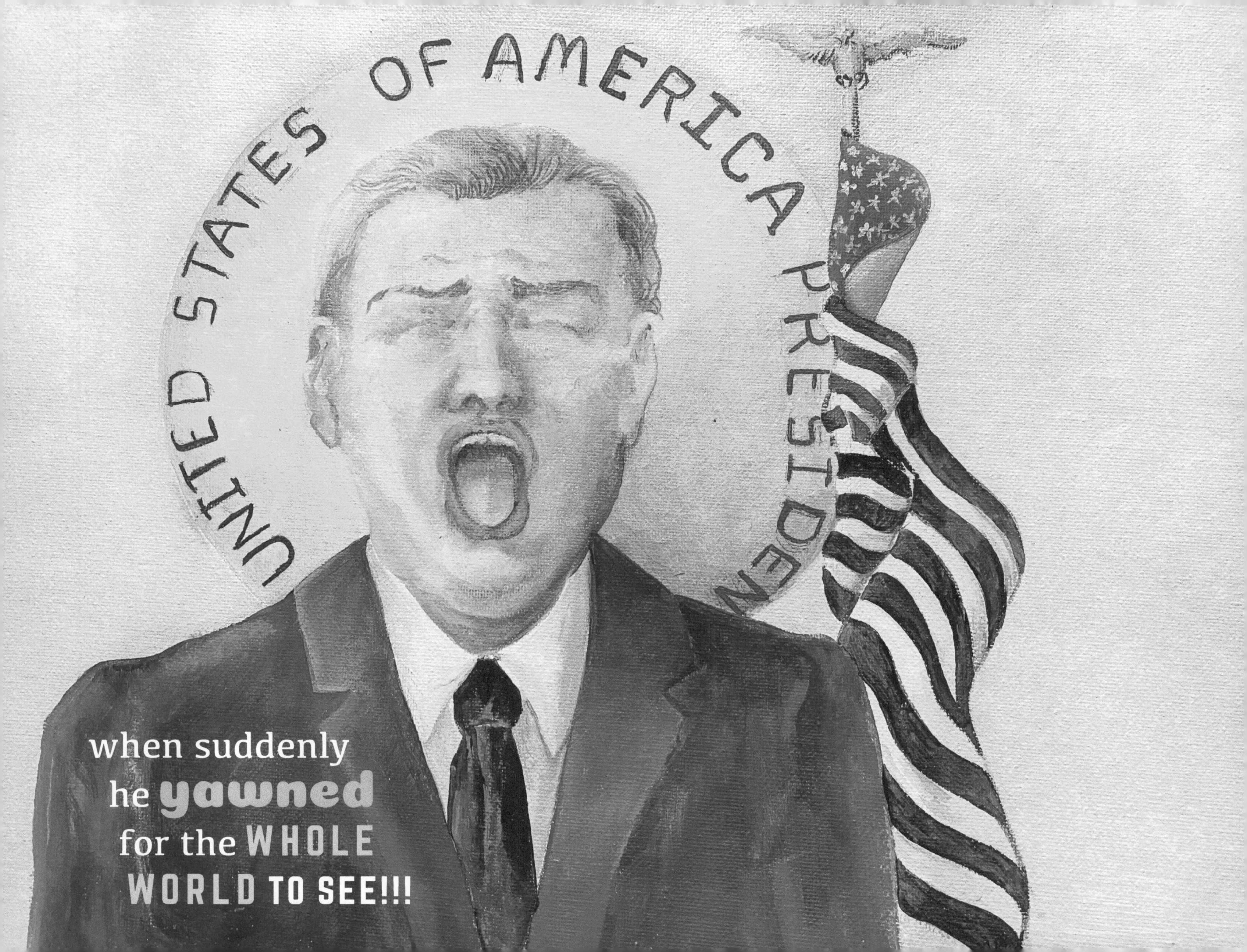

when suddenly
he **yawned**
for the **WHOLE**
WORLD TO SEE!!!

A few weeks later, back in the car,
Mommy and I weren't going too far.

I'd missed my nap, so tired was I,
that I **yawned really BIG**…

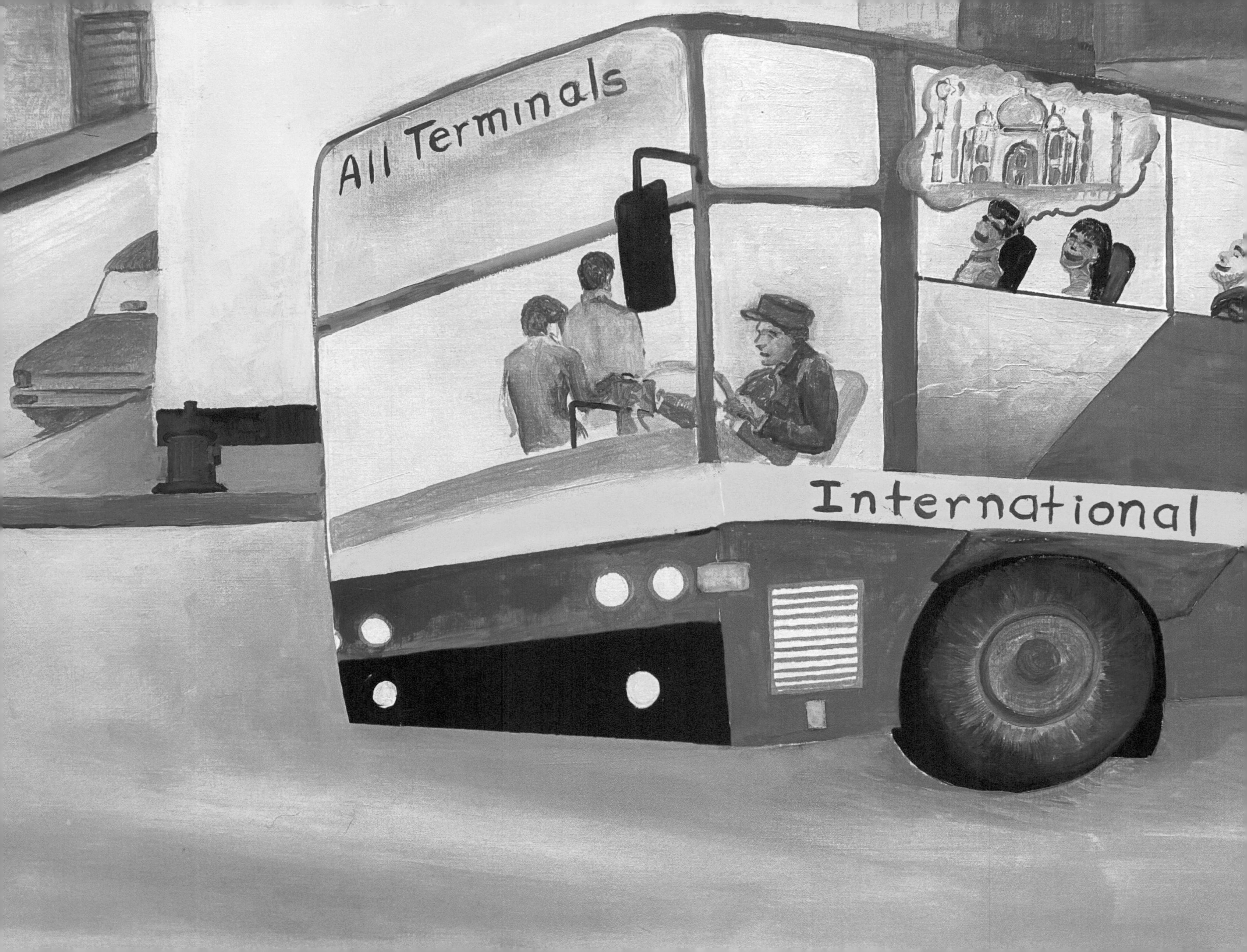
All Terminals
International

Airport

as a
BUS
sped
by!!!!

As I covered my mouth,
I could see Mommy smile.
The lesson was learned,
though it
took
me
a
while.

If **one single yawn** traveled so many miles, think what I'd do with **just one** of my **smiles!**

A yawn or a smile takes a trip every day. **Cover your yawns** and give SMILES away!

About the Authors

Patty Labriola grew up in Brooklyn, New York, and graduated from Fashion Institute of Technology. While working in the fashion industry, she became part of an entrepreneurial team in her early twenties, coaching others in business ownership. Her joy is found in surrounding herself with family, friends, and of course, children, many of whom inspire her creativity.

The Yawn that Went Around the World is Patty's first book and collaboration with longtime friends and business associates, Dayna and Kathleen. Patty lives in Fort Salonga, New York with her husband, Dennis. Their daughters, Christy and Stephanie, along with their son-in-law, Kevin, and granddaughters Emily, Beth, Kayla, and Jessica, turn the ordinary into the extraordinary.

Dayna Pappalardo is a former residential and commercial designer whose passion has always been to create and visualize beauty. Looking through the innocent eyes and imagination of children has enabled her to transfer her creativity into words. Dayna believes that children are the light needed to spread sunshine and happiness. Dayna says, "As you dance through life, the many songs you sing will be a reflection of the music inside you. People don't really care about what we say. They care about how the song we live makes them feel. My goal is for my song to inspire others to find the missing notes in their personal life melody."

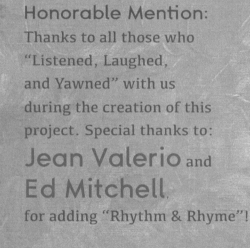

Honorable Mention:
Thanks to all those who "Listened, Laughed, and Yawned" with us during the creation of this project. Special thanks to:

Jean Valerio and
Ed Mitchell,
for adding "Rhythm & Rhyme"!

Kathleen Gurchie has enjoyed decades of success in her art painting business, serving many publications and numerous high-profile clients. Kathleen serves on the Board of the Art League of Long Island, and gives back to the art community in many ways. Kathleen believes, "One of the great joys of being an artist is to help others' vision come true. God created each of us to be unique, and in working together all of our gifts are magnified." She lives in Lindenhurst, New York with her husband, Al.

A free ebook edition is available with the purchase of this book.

To claim your free ebook edition:

1. Visit MorganJamesBOGO.com
2. Sign your name CLEARLY in the space
3. Complete the form and submit a photo of the entire copyright page
4. You or your friend can download the ebook to your preferred device

Morgan James BOGO™

A **FREE** ebook edition is available for you or a friend with the purchase of this print book.

_____

CLEARLY SIGN YOUR NAME ABOVE

Instructions to claim your free ebook edition:
1. Visit MorganJamesBOGO.com
2. Sign your name CLEARLY in the space above
3. Complete the form and submit a photo of this entire page
4. You or your friend can download the ebook to your preferred device

Print & Digital Together Forever.

Snap a photo

Free ebook

Read anywhere

CPSIA information can be obtained
at www.ICGtesting.com
Printed in the USA
LVHW011028021122
732106LV00003B/3